This book belongs to:

....

Text copyright © 2003 by Jeanne Willis. Illustrations copyright © 2003 by Tony Ross.
This paperback edition first published in 2005 by Andersen Press Ltd.
The rights of Jeanne Willis and Tony Ross to be identified as the author and illustrator of this
work have been asserted by them in accordance with the Copyright, Designs and Patents Act, 1988.
First published in Great Britain in 2003 by Andersen Press Ltd., 20 Vauxhall Bridge Road, London SW1V 2SA.
Published in Australia by Random House Australia Pty., 20 Alfred Street,Milsons Point, Sydney, NSW 2061.
Colour separated in Switzerland by Photolitho AG, Zürich. Printed and bound in Singapore.

10   9   8   7   6   5   4   3   2

British Library Cataloguing in Publication Data available.

ISBN 1 84270 463 X
This book has been printed on acid-free paper and is typeset in Century Schoolbook (of course!)

I hate School

Jeanne Willis / Tony Ross

Andersen Press
London

There was a fine young lady
And her name was Honor Brown,
She didn't want to go to school,
She hoped it would burn down.

And when I asked the child why,
Her little face turned red.
She threw her school hat on the floor
And this is what she said:

"My teacher is a warty toad!
My classroom is a hole!

The dinner ladies feed us worms,

And rabbit-poo and coal!"

And I believed her, every word —
For why should Honor lie?
And cling to mother on the step,

And stamp her feet and cry?

Weren't the lessons lots of fun?
And had she learnt to read?

"Oh, no," she said, "we don't do that,
They beat us till we bleed!

They throw us out of windows
And they make us walk on glass,

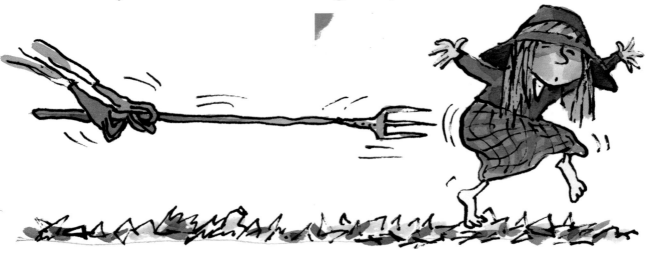

They always cut your head off
If you're talking in the class."

No wonder that she made a fuss
And didn't want to go –
But surely she had lovely friends?
Young Honor Brown cried, "No!

My friends are crooks and villains,
They are pirates! They are bad!

They are scary, spooky creatures,
They are monsters! They are mad!

They tied me to a rocket
And they sent me into space . . ."

No wonder little Honor Brown
Had such a grumpy face!

But what about the sandpit,
And the nice blue water tray?

"It would be fun," she said.
"If I could ever get to play.

The sandpit is a smelly swamp,
We sit in it and sink!

The water tray has sharks in,
They are killer sharks I think."

"Thank heavens for P.E.," I said.
"You love to swing on rope."
"Not by my neck I don't!" she said.
"Until I'm dead, they hope!"

Other titles written by Jeanne Willis
and illustrated by Tony Ross:

The Boy Who Lost His Bellybutton

Don't Let Go!

I Want To Be A Cowgirl

Manky Monkey

Misery Moo

Sloth's Shoes

Susan Laughs

Tadpole's Promise

What Did I Look Like When I Was A Baby?

~ ~ ~

And don't miss . . .

the Dr Xargle series including

Dr Xargle's Book of Earthlets

. . . from the same partnership!